The Mystery of Him
Book 2 of The Taslasness Chronicles

The Mystery of Him
Book 2 of The Taslasness Chronicles
Kevin James Keyser

Kevin James Keyser

2014

Acknowledgements

I would like to thank the following people for their help and support:

- Tina Struck – Editor and Proofreader
- Jim Struck – Story flow
- Taly Reznik – Cover Art

The Storm

Thunder and a flash of light. Is she dreaming? She must be dreaming. It never thunders here. The rains are always long, soaking and gentle. They are never, ever violent. Yet the thunder comes again - this time with wind and a bright flash. Delineni opened her eyes.

There was a storm outside! The trees were leaning in the wind, the rain was pelting the house and all the windows were open.

Delineni got out of bed and ran through the thatched roofed house shutting all the windows and drawing in the seldom-to-never used shutters.

The cat was hiding under the table in the parlor. Delineni looked at him:

"Where is Dad? What's going on?"

The cat shuddered as thunder and instantaneous lightning revealed her father's image through the window. He was on one of the near by hills, his staff held high in the sky and he had just deflected a lightning bolt!

That was enough for Delineni. Wizard or not, this is dangerous and he shouldn't be out there. She threw on a cape and ran out the door to get him.

She was no more then several steps out the door when the hail started; big, golf ball size hail.

Taslasness turned towards his daughter, his staff pointed towards her as she winced in pain from the many hail balls.

His voice echoed through out all the land:

"Protect!"

A bubble of golden energy formed around her, stopping the hail and rain from getting to her.

Taslasness raised the staff and his left hand:

"Enough! Into the outer realm I call forth Lightener to set the world right!"

There was huge release of energy. Delineni saw bursts of white, blue, green then she felt a terrible thud and everything went dark.

"She's coming around," an unknown voice said.

"She has a will of steel!" Taslasness said.

Delineni opened her eyes and blinked. She was in her bedroom. Taslasness was holding her hands and someone wearing a white robe was standing in back of him. The other man looked older then Taslasness. He was tall, clean shaven, balding, with a golden skullcap.

"Father?" She blinked again, winced in pain as she started to get up. "What happened?"

"Shhh, Shhh, now Delineni. Take it easy."

"Ow! What hit me?"

The other man walked towards her: "That would be me, child."

"What? Who are you?"

"I am Lightener, the eldest Wizard. Your father was my student years and years ago."

"What do you mean you hit me?"

Lightener sighed: "When your father called me the situation was desperate, so I opened the nearest portal and rushed to his aid. Unfortunately you were between him and me."

"You must have been moving quickly because the hail didn't even make a dent in that bubble thing."

"I believe I was moving at 1/3 the speed of light, child."

"That's really fast."

Taslasness was still steadying Delineni until she shook his hand off.

"Is someone going to tell me what's going on?"

Lightener nodded his head: "Nebulzar has returned."

Delineni scratched her head: "Who?"

Music's End

The next day found the sky bright, a gentle breeze blowing through the Land Of Wonder. Delineni, Taslasness and Lightener were walking towards the River of Life.

"So who is this Nebulzar you were talking about yesterday?"

Taslasness smiled: "Who?"

Delineni got indignant: "Father! I know you made me fall asleep when I asked before. Just tell me who he is and why he made it storm so much."

Taslasness shook his head and sighed: "You are much too clever for your own good."

Taslasness started to cast out the net to catch the day's idea fishes, the songs still un-sung when they all saw it at the same time.

Delineni screamed - Lightener put his hand over his mouth. Taslasness just stood there flushed with anger.

The idea fishes were all dead.

Taslasness spoke, enraged: "You want to know who Nebulzar is? Now you have your answer! Nebulzar is the evil one, the eater of love, the prince of gluttony, the destroyer of creativity and all that springs forth from it."

Lightener put his hand on Taslasness's shoulder: "We thought him banished eons ago but he and his pet have somehow returned."

"Pet?"

"He calls it the Pig of Death. It's not just one pig as he slaughters many, often in ritual."

"He kills them?!"

"Yes, and the energy derived from their death is used to power his various machinations. He probably slaughtered one last night to attack your Father and kill the idea fish."

Delineni walked to her father: "What can we do?"

Taslasness touched her head: "I think Lightener and I need to counsel on this for a while. Lightener has a few special talents that will help."

"Oh?"

Lightener smiles: "I am the gatekeeper for time and light."

"Huh? I don't speak the same language you do, I guess."

Lightener looked almost hurt: "I can open gates not only to places, like you can. I can open gates to the when and the will be. The past and the future."

Taslasness smiled: "Do you see how helpful this would be?"

Delineni nodded: "He can go anywhere. He can go back if we fail and try again."

Lightener nodded: "Within some limits, yes."

"What limits?"

Taslasness motioned to Lightener to keep quiet: "We can't tell you now Delineni, it's already too dangerous for you here. That knowledge would make you a bigger target."

"Oh let that Nebulzar try something else, Dad! I'll beam him to the center of the Earth."

"Leave the Earth out of this; they are messed up enough as it is!"

Lightener put his hand on Taslasness's shoulder: "Earth! That might be a perfect place to go to for a while, Delineni."

"What?! I'm not leaving my Father!"

Taslasness nodded: "I think it may not be safe here for a while, daughter. Why don't you go back to the house on Land Avenue for a while?"

"Dad, that place is a dump!"

"Oh, you and Kaswan can clean it up."

Lightener smiled: "Oh, yes, Kaswan. I heard of him."

Delineni frowned: "He's just a human male."

Lightener nodded: "One that you keep drawing pictures of, I hear."

Delineni blushed: "I find him an interesting specimen, that's all!"

Taslasness smiled: "It's settled then, off you go. Lightener will open a gate and then seal all gates until this is resolved."

"No, Dad! If he seals the gates I'll be stuck there!"

"Yes, and Nebulzar won't be able to get to you either."

"But!"

"No buts!"

Lightener pointed his medallion towards Delineni, there was a flash of golden light and Delineni found herself once again in the old, dilapidated yellow brick house on Land Avenue.

The gate in the mirror closed, for the first time with an audible "frump" sound. She tried to open it and couldn't.

It looked to be raining outside. Pouring actually. Delineni felt something wet touch her head. She looked up to see the roof leaking on her: "Great, just great!"

Face of Evil

"That was "Magic" by the Scottish pop rock band Pilot. Number 61 on the US Billboard Hot 100 list for September 18, 1975!"

Someone had a radio playing as Keith Newheart, a sophomore at Eastern High School, walked up to the rusting, brown metal doors on his way to the first class of the day. As he walked, he passed two seniors he had seen before. The male was tall and had red hair, the female shorter with blond hair. It was hard to tell much else about them because they were always locking lips. One could never get a good look at either of them.

Keith shook his head and muttered: "Seniors!"

Moments later a shadowy, hooded man walked in the building pausing to look at the couple. In his hand he held a medallion which pulsated red.

The man walked, more like floated, through the entire building several times as though looking for someone or something. No one noticed him, no one even thought to notice him. It's as though every time someone might have seen him they thought of looking in the opposite direction before they could.

That was before the figure entered the classroom Keith was in.

Keith was seated taking notes when all of a sudden he started to feel sick to his stomach. He felt drained of energy, cold. He looked up and saw something impossible. A hooded man passed through the door looked around and then snapped his head to Keith's location and gazed at him. The man's medallion quickly flashed red.

Horrified, Keith looked around. No one else seemed to even notice what was going on. The man floated towards Keith and then stood next to him. In his head a gravelly voice barked words to him:

"You have been there."

Keith wanted to speak but couldn't open his mouth.

"I Hear your thoughts, mortal."

Keith thought back to the creature: "Where have I been?"

Keith started to see pictures in his head of the wizard Taslasness and his daughter, Delineni. He had dreamt of them last year and then written some stories about their supposed adventures.

The man pulled back and angrily growled the words "It was no dream! You have been there but are not from there. How is this possible?"

He peered in to Keith's eyes. After a moment it looked as though he realized he would get nothing more from Keith. He moved back and then wasn't there anymore.

Keith, now able to move, stood up in class. The teacher paused as he started to run out of the room. He only got as far as the next desk when he lost it, vomiting on everything except the surprised classmate, who jumped out of the way.

A few minutes later Keith found himself on a cot in the school nurse's office.

"How are you doing sweetie?" Keith's mother smiled as she walked in.

Keith sat up: "I'm sick to my stomach, Mom. Kind of woozy."

The nurse patted him on the head: "You have been drinking too much pop and not enough water."

His mother helped him up: "Come on sweetie, we are going to see the doctor."

"Mom, I don't want to see the doctor, he's a weirdo."

"I don't care! We are going to see the doctor!"

Keith realized that there was no escape and sighed: "OK."

His mother picked up his books, and they walked out of the nurse's office.

"What were you doing right before you got sick?"

"Just listening to the teacher talking about some Irish legend, then I felt sick."

Keith sure wasn't going to tell anyone about the hooded dude.

The nurse followed them to the door of her office." Mrs. Newheart; Really too much pop and not enough water!"

Keith's mother turned and looked at the nurse; Keith swore the room got really cold as they walked out.

Hours later Keith found himself in his bedroom with a pitcher of ice water, a vaporizer and Vicks VapoRub.

The hour was late, everyone else was asleep but Keith couldn't. Not with all these thoughts of the creature and how sick he felt flooding his mind.

The light in the room turned a golden hue the same light Keith dreamt of a year ago. A brilliant shaft appeared in front of him and out stepped Delineni:

"I think its name is Nebulzar."

Keith stared in disbelief: "It's true, you are real! I thought you were a dream!"

Delineni saw the now-dried up mood orchid that he had picked during their previous time together on his night stand. She took it in her hand: "If I was just a dream, why keep part of the dream next to you?"

Keith smiled: "Um, it was a good dream?"

Delineni put the mood orchid back down: "I'm real, Kaswan. Do you remember that Kaswan is your given name?"

Keith/Kaswan smiled and took out a notebook from the shelf next to the bed:

"Sure I do, I wrote all these stories with you and me in them!"

She picked up the notebook and read a passage about herself:

"Delineni had long, strawberry blond hair, a bow of gold, and a duck!"

Delineni laughed and threw the notebook back to him: "A bow of gold and a duck!"

"Well, it seemed cool at the time!"

Keith/Kaswan's smile disappeared: "What is this Nebulzar?"

Delineni looked as though she was a balloon, just deflated. She sat on the foot of his bed and over the next hour or two told him everything she knew.

Keith shook his head: "So you can't go home?"

"No, I can travel between places here but all the gates back home are blocked to me."

She almost looked like she was going to cry. This was a side of Delineni Keith had never seen previously. She always seemed to be so in control, so sure of herself. Now this mystical girl was sitting on the foot of his bed and she looked alone, frightened and tired.

A realization came into Keith's head: "Delineni! He was looking for you, wasn't he? Nebulzar was looking for you!"

She shrugged: "I guess so. I think he followed you, Keith, because once you cross over to the Land of Wonder it leaves a mark on you that others can see if they know what to look for. He probably sensed that a gate had opened and someone passed through it. I think he mistook you for me."

"Then you are in danger."

"So it would seem. Funny, Dad and Lightener sent me here and locked the gates to keep me safe, thinking that Nebulzar would stay in the Land of Wonder. I guess they hadn't thought that Nebulzar was already on Earth."

"Is there a way I could get in touch with Taslasness so he knows that Nebulzar is here?"

Delineni brightened: "You know, there may be a way."

"Well, lets get to work then."

"Not now, I'll see you tomorrow. You need to sleep."

"But what if he..."

Delineni kissed Keith/Kaswan on his cheek and he fell instantly to sleep.

She whispered: "He can't find what he can't see." She turned back in golden light and then jumped into a nearby light bulb."

The Pig of Death

It looked like a floating black disc, just under a mile in diameter. It was more than black, in fact light didn't emanate from it at all. Light was absorbed by it.

In the middle of the disc was a structure made out of what looked to be spider legs but was, in fact, thin metal tubes. The metal tubes connected to a large black metal plate. Upon the plate was a holding pen filled with pigs, a chair and a table.

The hooded figure of Nebulzar paced back and forth talking, out loud as if to the pigs:

"It's almost in place, yes. See you not! All these years and I can finally purge the universe of these emotional fools! Without their love, hate, writing, music, worship, art and creativity the Land of Wonder will cease to exist!"

One could swear that he laughed when saying this, but laughter would be an emotion and therefore a weakness.

"That would be the end of Taslasness and all those other so called "wizards" who stood in the way before! The universe abhors a vacuum; the first step is to replace all that creativity with something else."

He took a dagger out of his pocket and started to poke one the caged pigs with it:

"We must make them want. We must make them want everything of a material value, nothing of a creative or spiritual value. It must become self perpetuating, they will know they are missing something and try to fill that void with more and more material things."

He opened the cage door and pulled one little pig out by its neck.

"I know just how to do it."

The dagger came down in one quick move; the pig squealed loudly and then became forever silent.

His hands were covered in pig's blood. The hands glowed red as he chanted something that can not be written without changing the words as they are wrote.

Below in town, it started to rain. A strange rain, a strange smell and a strange feeling washed over the populace below.

Nebulzar neither smiled, nor frowned. He was completely devoid of any emotion.

Yet if one was to glance upon his face, one might somehow think he was pleased, quite pleased.

Out of the corner of his eye he saw, just for a second, a flash of golden light. He turned to get a better look and it was gone. He turned back, chanting the changeable words, hands still glowing red.

Delineni hovered near one of the sickly orange streetlights so as to hide herself.

She was horrified at the sight, the smell and the growing realization that something was wrong with the people below. Something she couldn't put her finger on, but something screaming from the back of her mind with danger.

In her mind she was again a young child. Her mother, Tal'shire was running with Delineni. There was this strange smell, the same one she smelled now.

Delineni cried, remembering the last time she saw her mother alive and realizing for the first time that Nebulzar had something to do with her death.

On the black disc was a large empty glass globe. Attached to the glass globe going all the way around its equator were what looked like metal, glowing leeches.

The metal leeches somehow squirmed and pulsed as the globe slowly filled with a red, sticky substance. Not blood but like blood.

Pure and refined.

That which was stolen from those below.

The dreams, the thoughts of a better tomorrow, the music no longer heard in their minds. The visions, once colorful and now grey, lifeless.

No smiles shown or felt. Those below, within the range of Nebulzar, wandered around as if looking for something lost. As if they were lost.

For they were.

The metal leaches continued to pump the liquefied elixir of wonder in to the globe. The static-induced smell of ozone continued to fill the air.

Delineni felt something she never thought possible. She felt as if a part of her was being tampered with. She materialized and was instantly swept over by despair and wanting. Wanting for what, she wondered?

She grabbed the lamp pole and steadied herself. She reached in to her pocket and without knowing what she was doing grabbed hold of her golden medallion. The symbol of the Triad glowed bright. She inhaled like she was starved for air, but it wasn't air she needed.

Out of the corner of his eye Nebulzar saw another golden flash. He turned around to find out what caused it at the same time Delineni's medallion opened a gate and pulled Delineni through it.

Nebulzar saw none of this but it put him on guard, so with a snap of his fingers the entire disc disappeared from the Earth and returned back to his hiding place deep in Earth's moon.

There was an audible shudder that came from the people who were tampered with. They felt as though a fog was lifting from their minds. They felt drained of energy, they felt alone.

Some went home; some no longer knew or cared what home was.

In the house on Land Avenue, Delineni laid unconscious and shivering on the floor. The huge mirror she had just past through went cold, silent and dark.

The Bottomless Will

The rain was poured down, lightning flashed, thunder rumbled. Keith Newheart stirred in his bed. His eyes opened, focused on the silent alarm clock. It was 3:13 AM Saturday morning and something was wrong.

A feeling of dread filled Keith in a way he had never felt before. In his mind he saw the haunted house. He had to go there; he had to go there right away.

He fought the feeling as illogical or the remnant of a dream he couldn't remember. He sure wasn't going to **that** house in the wee hours! The feeling persisted and he couldn't take it anymore. "Mom's going to kill me" he mouthed.

He dressed himself, put his rubber rain poncho on, grabbed his flashlight and snuck down the stairs. So far he wasn't busted! He opened the door as a huge thunder clap sounded. He looked around, no one woke up. He closed the door silently and ran down Land Avenue towards the haunted house.

The haunted house loomed up in the storm. He ran up the cracked concrete stairs and found the door boarded up. Someone had done this since the last time Delineni and he were there.

He pulled at the boards and they gave way, he pushed the door open and worked his way to the front room. The flashlight revealed Delineni on the floor, still unconscious.

"Delineni? My God, what happened?" She didn't move or make a sound.

He touched her face and she was freezing cold. He pulled some of the sheets off the furniture, shook the dust off them and piled them on top of Delineni. He found a pillow under the sheets on the couch and put it under her head.

Just then he saw a soft golden pulse of light coming from Delineni's hand. It was the golden medallion which pulsed softly.

"I don't know what to do, Delineni. I'm going to get Mom and Dad. Maybe there's a Doctor around or something."

As Keith got up to leave, the medallion became very bright and steady. Keith opened her hand and then took both her hand and the medallion in to his. There was a very bright light and then the sound of chirping birds.

Keith shook his head and looked at his watch, it was 8:00! "How did it become 8:00? It was just 3 something a second ago!"

Keith was now convinced that his parents were going to kill him.

Delineni opened her eyes.

"What? Um, Kaswan is that you?"

"Hey."

"What happened?"

"I don't know. I felt I had to come here, like hours ago. I found you here; you were shivering and knocked out. I covered you up; put that old pillow under your head. I noticed that your medallion was flashing on and off. I looked at it and it became very bright. I felt like I had to, well..."

Keith was blushing.

"Hold my hand?" Delineni said, finishing his sentence.

"Yeah. Then I looked around and it was 8:00 in the morning!"

"Thank you, Kaswan."

"For what?"

"Saving me."

"Saving you?"

"When my medallion is flashing like that it means I'm injured, I'm injured badly. It asked you if you could help me by giving a few hours of your life to heal me."

"Nothing asked me anything."

"It's not words, it's feelings."

"Well, I did feel like I should hold your hand."

"And you did."

"Then it became morning, 8:00 in the morning. Mom and Dad are going to kill me!"

"No they won't. They think you are still sleeping."

"They check the room."

"Not today, they didn't."

"How do you know?"

"I just know."

Keith sighed. "Are you alright?"

"I need to rest, come back tonight and we'll talk, OK?"

"But…"

Delineni had closed her eyes and drifted off to sleep. Keith walked back home, through the door and back upstairs. Once in bed a couple minutes, his mother opened the door.

"Oh good, you are awake. How are you doing sweetie?"

Keith wasn't lying when he told her he was really, really tired.

"You rest up; you had a bad day yesterday. I'll go with your father shopping."

"Thanks, Mom."

She kissed him on the forehead and walked out of the room.

Keith's eyes became heavy as he fell in to a long and deep sleep.

The sun was orange and low as Keith woke up.

"I slept the whole day?!" Keith mouthed out loud as he realized that it was almost night.

His mother knocked on the door.

"Come In"

"How are you feeling?"

"A lot better, Mom. I can't believe that I slept the whole day away."

"You were sick that's why, sweetie."

"I guess, but I'm better now. Can I go out?"

His mother laughed: "No way! Just watch TV or something. If you are still feeling better tomorrow you can get your homework done."

"I don't have any homework."

His mother smiled: "Yes you do, your homeroom teacher dropped off the homework from all your classes, so you won't miss anything."

"But Mom, I'm sick!"

"Nice try, Keith!"

Keith laughed: "Can't blame me for trying!"

His mother got up and walked towards the door: "Your father is working tonight so I'll be right downstairs if you don't feel good."

"Ok."

She walked out of the room. Keith turned on his black and white TV set just in time to see the start of "Emergency!" "Least I didn't miss this."

"Miss what?"

Keith jumped at the sound of the disembodied voice.

"Oh I'm sorry; I forgot I was still hiding in a sunray!"

With that Delineni appeared standing by the window, seeming to jump out of the orange light coming from the setting sun.

"How long have you been here?"

With a wave of her hand Delineni turned up the volume on the TV.

"A while."

"Was I still asleep?"

"You snore."

"Hey!" Keith threw his pillow at her.

"Ewww! Get that away from me, you drool too!"

She threw the pillow back to Keith and they both laughed.

"Thank you, Kaswan."

"No biggie."

"Yes, biggie! What you did would have frightened almost anybody."

"I didn't know what I was doing."

Delineni just smiled her Cheshire cat smile.

The fire truck on TV was sounding its siren, responding to a fictional fire. Delineni sat on the foot of Keith's bed, watching the TV with him until the commercial break.

"How are you, Delineni?"

"Tired but OK."

"It was Nebulzar, wasn't it?"

"Yes and not just me, a bunch of people on the ground got sick as well. A couple of people might have died, I'm not sure."

"Died?!"

"It's like he sucked all the life out of them, but it was more than that. The people who weren't hurt enough to die lost something else."

"Something else?"

"It was like all joy left them, it was like anything creative left them and there was this longing feeling."

"I don't understand. How do you know what they were…?"

Keith realized that she was describing what happened to her, too. He sat up in bed and put his hand on her shoulder. She touched his hand for a moment, got up off of the foot of the bed and started to pace around the room.

"What was the longing for, Delineni?"

"Something to replace what they were now missing."

"What were they missing?"

Delineni kicked his waste basket across the room. "I don't know."

"Whoa! Mom will hear."

"She's asleep."

"You just know, right?"

Delineni smiled. "She snores too."

Kaswan laughed: "She does, how can you hear that from all the way up here?"

"You would be surprised at the stuff I can…"

Delineni stopped talking, put her finger up over her mouth and turned to look at the television.

"Shhh! Something's happening."

"I don't see any…" Keith's words trailed off as the television started to fade out to red.

The same gravelly voice that spoke to Keith in the classroom came through the television's speaker, starting with an animal like growl:

"Ah! You are Taslasness's child! I remember - you weren't yet three years old when I smote your mother."

Delineni got up off the bed and confronted the television:

"You! You're a monster!"

This would have been the time a typical villain would of laughed and gloated that yes, he was a monster. Gloating is an emotion and therefore a weakness. Instead he continued talking like Delineni never even said anything:

"I thought it was you after I tasted your essence in my latest harvest. How is it that you are still alive, child?"

Keith yelled: "Leave her alone!" Keith got out of the bed and unplugged the television. The red screen did not go away.

Nebulzar continued, again without showing any emotion:

"I see, you have a pet. Gave you some of his life did he now? Go home, Delineni. Go home and tell your father that he is beaten. Then watch as I take all the human's dreams, their hope, their love, their passions. Then see what I replace them with. See your Land of Wonder turn brown and die. Go home now or I kill you and your pet tomorrow night."

The television finally turned off. Delineni was about to say something when Keith's Mom's voice came through the door: "Keith! Turn that television down!"

Delineni held up her hand:

"Do you still have the medallion I gave you last year?"

Keith had a puzzle box on the shelf. He unlocked it with a couple twists and turns then took out the still glowing medallion.

Delineni smiled: "Tomorrow afternoon at the haunted house." She turned into light, flew out the window and followed the streetlights until she was out of view.

Keith shook his head and muttered to himself: "I'm a pet?"

Mirror, Mirror

"Keith, is you homework done?"

"Yes, Mom. Want to read it?"

"No. Ok, you can go but be back early, I don't want you showing up to school all tired and getting sick again."

Keith was out of the house almost before he said "OK."

It was late afternoon as he ran down to the haunted house, up its steps and opened its rickety door.

"Delineni?"

Her voice came from near the huge mirror: "Here".

Delineni was sitting on the floor. Her legs were crossed and her hands elevated palms up but tilted slightly towards each other. Above her hands but centered between them was a glowing ball of something.

Delineni extended one hand and the ball – something – hovered above it. Then she unwrapped her legs and got up.

Keith smiled: "That looks like it hurts!"

"No, it doesn't hurt at all."

Keith shrugged his shoulders:

"What's that glowing ball?"

"It's not a ball, it's an Orb"

"Orb?"

"Yeah, this one is a message Orb."

"What do you do with it?"

"Send messages, that why it's called a message orb, duh!"

"Ever hear of the post office??"

"The post office doesn't go where this is going."

"Oh, you found a way to get in touch with your Dad?"

"Yup, I'm looking right at it."

"Huh? You're looking at me."

"Exactly!"

"I thought you said the gates were closed."

"They are, to me."

"But not to me?"

"Nope."

"So you want me to take this thing.."

"Message Orb!"

"... Yeah, Message Orb, to your Dad?"

"Please, could you?"

Keith thought about it a moment or two:

"What do I do?"

Delineni held out the hand the orb was floating above and blew it over to Keith: "Let it float above you. Don't touch it until you see my father."

"Then what?"

"He will know what to do."

Keith regarded the floating orb above him and then looked back to Delineni:

"What are you going to do when I'm gone?"

She smiled: "I'm going hide out somewhere that I don't think Nebulzar knows about."

"Where?"

She looked a little sad: "I can't tell you, because even thinking about it could give it away."

"How do I find you when I come back?"

"I'll find you."

Keith nodded and took out the medallion: "I hold this to my heart, right?"

"You remember, good! Then walk through the mirror"

Keith smiled: "This better work, I don't want 7 years bad luck!"

"It will work!"

Keith held the medallion to his chest and walked through the mirror like it was thin air.

Delineni smiled and then frowned. She became a different kind of light. Blue, white with shades of grey. She flew in an electrical outlet. The haunted house was empty again.

Kaswan found himself standing on a hill. He turned around to see the gate just shutting with a "thump" sound.

Where was he, he wondered. The hill that he was on last year was green, lush and full of life. This hill had brown grass, the surrounding trees were leafless. The temperature was cool; there was the rattle of thunder in the distance.

Kaswan could see that there was a river about 3 miles away and on the bank, near a bend in the river, was a thatched roof house. It was then Kaswan realized that he was standing on the same hill as a year before. Yes, something was wrong with the "Land of Wonder", and he knew who was causing it. Kaswan looked above him and the Message Orb was still there. He headed down the hill and towards the house.

Halfway down the hill he saw a flash out of the corner of his eye. What looked like slow motion lightning was heading for the tree next to him. He jumped away from the tree just as it hit it. The tree wasn't there anymore, just a pile of ash remained. He realized that even lightning wouldn't do that. There was another flash; another bolt was heading his way. Kaswan realized that he was under attack and started to run towards the house.

This time a boulder was turned to dust. Kaswan ran as fast as possible. Another flash caught the corner of his eye and then a big booming voice echoed through the land: "Protect!"

A bubble of golden energy formed around Kaswan and then there was a brilliant flash as the bolt hit the bubble, cracking it and throwing Kaswan on to the ground.

Taslasness ran up, grabbed Kaswan by the arm and the world turned inside out. Everything looked like iron fillings placed on a piece of paper and then moved around by a magnet.

Then Kaswan realized that they were in the house. Taslasness was looking down at him and another man was standing in back of Taslasness.

Taslasness smiled and helped Kaswan to his feet: "That was exciting, wasn't it?"

Kaswan shook his head: "Nebulzar was trying to kill me!"

"No, that wasn't Nebulzar. Just one of his pigs."

"Pigs?"

Lightener stepped up: "I am Lightener."

"Hi, I'm Kei… I mean, I'm Kaswan."

Taslasness reached out and took the message orb. Kaswan had actually forgotten it was there:

"We have been waiting for this."

"Delineni said you would know what to do with it."

Taslasness said nothing but took the message orb and shoved it in to his chest. He sat down on the chair and rocked.

Lightener put a finger to his lips and motioned Kaswan to the other room. He whispered:

"It takes a while for the message to soak in."

Kaswan nodded. "You guys were expecting me?"

"You are a smart one! Delineni chooses her friends well."

"I don't understand."

Taslasness got up out of the chair: "We can't track Nebulzar, he would have been aware of our attempts. We needed someone to find out what he was up to. Someone who he wouldn't detect, at least right away."

"You didn't send Delineni to earth to protect her, you planned to send her!"

Taslasness nodded: "It was the only way."

Kaswan grew angry: "She could have died."

"Yes, but we knew you would be there."

"Me?"

Taslasness walked over to Kaswan and put his hand on his shoulder:

"Thank you for saving her."

"I didn't know what I was doing."

"Yes you did, you just didn't know what you knew."

"Taslasness, why do you always make my head hurt?"

Taslasness smiled: "I hear this often! Kaswan, there are things I can't tell you now because they could ruin your future. Lightener over there sees the future. There is one, you know."

Kaswan laughed: "Ok, then what can you tell me? How can we help Delineni and get rid of Nebulzar?"

"Let's break bread and talk."

They all sat at the table. Taslasness poured some kind of honey flavored drink and served bread with some kind of cheese.

Lightener finished some cheese then took an orb out of nowhere. He tossed the orb in the air. There was a flash and pictures are displayed, floating above the table. The pictures moved.

"What is this, TV?"

Taslasness shook his head: "It's like TV. Close enough for our purposes."

Two of the people pictured look familiar to Kaswan: "I think I know those people."

Lightener nodded his head: "They go to the same school you do."

"They do?"

Kaswan looked really close at the "TV". The unhappy couple were in a store buying a lot of useless junk. Not even talking to each other much. They were spending a lot of money.

"Wait a minute. Those are the two seniors I always see kissing in the hallway. I never even see their faces. They are always so happy and so full of each other. It can't be the same people."

Taslasness finishes his bread: "Oh yes, it is the same couple. Their sense of wonder has been stolen from them. Now they look to replace something they feel as missing with, how did you say? A lot of useless junk."

"You can't replace a feeling with stuff."

"If you are desperate you try anything."

"Taslasness, my head hurts again!"

Lightener laughed: "Buying stuff gives people a temporary sense of satisfaction. When they are missing everything else, this fills the void."

"But love is an energy. Taslasness, you made my head hurt last year explaining this to me."

Taslasness nodded: "But all energy can be harvested and used for other purposes."

"Really? Like its coal or oil or something?"

"Exactly."

"But these are living people, not some old dead dinosaur!"

The two wizards nodded as Kaswan continued:

"What does he do with the energy?"

Taslasness shook his head: "He uses it to power his various machinations. He uses it to renew himself, to almost obtain immortality."

"That's horrible!"

Lightener nodded: "Yes it is. That's why we must stop this."

"How?"

Taslasness put the cheese away: "Oh we have a plan, but we need your help."

"What can I do?"

Taslasness smiled: "I'm going to give you a message orb to take back to Delineni. Give it to her and she will know what to do and where to go."

"OK, do I need to walk through the forest to get back to the gate?"

Lightener stood up, pointed his staff at the wall which shimmered: "I am the gate keeper for time and light. I get to create gates anywhere!"

"I walk through this and I'm where?"

"Your bedroom."

Kaswan nodded, sighed and walked through the gate. Lightener closed the gate behind him and this time he sealed it with a wave of his hands: "There. It is done, Taslasness."

Taslasness sat down on his chair. His cat jumped up in his lap: "All the pieces are in place."

Lightener sighed: "Now it's Nebulzar's move."

Taslasness waved all but one of the candles out. The two wizards sat alone and said nothing else.

Remember?

The Faelands, an island kingdom in another dimension. A woman and a child run out of a cave, one of the Omri caves. The woman holds her daughter's hand as they scurry down the steep slope. In back of them the cave, which moments ago was dark, now has a deep red glow from within.

Out from the cave emerges Nebulzar. "Tal'Shire!" He screamed, his words booming throughout the land.

He twists and turns until he sees them running away. He dematerialized and then reappeared in front of the mother and daughter.

He raised his dagger, clenched hard in his fist and stabbed Tal'Shire in the heart.

A noise woke Delineni up from this dream and she screamed. She looked outside of the electrical outlet in time to see Keith/Kaswan jumping out of what looked to be a temporary gate.

"Lightener" she whispered, shaking her head.

There was a message orb floating above Keith. Delineni got ready to transform from energy to physical form just as Keith whispered her name.

There was a buzzing sound as Delineni jumped out of the electrical outlet.

Keith jumped back: "Wow! I've never seen you do that before!"

Delineni said nothing; she just smiled, took the message orb from Keith and pushed it into her chest. Then she sat down on Keith's bed and let the message soak in, Keith silently sitting beside her.

In the moon, under "Lacus Oblivionis" was a huge circular cavern, almost 30 miles in diameter. A cavern somehow filled with a mix of oxygen, nitrogen and various other gases. In the middle of that cavern sat Nebulzar's black disc. The walls of the cavern gave off a greenish, luminescent glow.

On the disc, below the pig pen a machine of some kind showed a gold indicator and made a gentle beeping sound. Nebulzar walked to the machine, taped a button and the indicator went dark, the beeping stopped. No one else besides him and the pigs were there. Still, he talked aloud:

"Another crossover indication; It looks as though she has returned."

He climbed up the metal spider legs to the top disc, sat in his chair.

"She is like her mother, she won't listen to reason. I will have to kill her sooner than I wanted." He went to another machine and turned on various switches and dials.

Back in Keith's room Delineni finally said: "I see."

"What do you see, Delineni?"

"I see what we are going to do and where we are going to do it."

She paused and Keith could see she was also rather upset:

"Does it scare you?"

She shrugged: "A little."

"Where are we going Delineni?"

She looked at him in a way he had never seen anyone look at him before. She was melancholy, but her eyes hid something else. Something Keith would only figure out years in the future.

"I'm going to a place called the Faelands, then from there to Ireland."

"You? I'm going too."

"It's really dangerous."

Keith laughed: "I almost got blown up today! I think it can't get much more dangerous then that!"

She held his hand and he blushed. She smiled: "You don't have to come but I'd be happy to have you at my side."

Delineni saw the television start to glow red just as Keith asked: "When do we go?"

She held his hand very hard and whispered, "Now!"

The world turned inside out for Keith. He saw that he was traveling along side Delineni. They were both beams of light traveling at the speed of light. The world passed below them and then dissolved in to a black nothingness, which gave way to a purple vortex and then a cave.

Delineni let go of his hand: "We have a few minutes before Nebulzar follows. This is one of the Omri Caves. They are said to be time travel caves but they are much more than that. These caves are natural gates to multiple dimensions."

Keith smiled: "Including the Land of Wonder?"

Delineni nodded: "Yeah. One also leads to the Giant's Causeway."

"What's that?"

"It's a place in Northern Ireland. Its unique geology will give us an advantage. Now we need to get ready."

There was a golden glow. The whole cavern lit up. A circle appeared in the middle of the cavern and from the circle stepped Taslasness and Lightener.

"Father!" Delineni ran up and took her father in her arms.

Lightener walked to Keith/Kaswan: "Very good! We have to wait here until Nebulzar shows himself. Then we lead him to the Causeway."

Kaswan nodded: "So Delineni tells me. Then what?"

Lightener smiled: "Then we hope he attacks."

Lightener patted a very surprised Kaswan on the back and walked back to Taslasness and Delineni: "He will be here soon, I can smell it."

Taslasness motioned Kaswan to come to him. Then they all joined hands. Kaswan laughed: "So, what, we are all bait?"

Delineni wacked him on the head: "Not bait, we are an enticement!" Her smile left her mouth as the room turned red.

Then Nebulzar appeared. He was floating on a small black disc in front of them. The small disc was only large enough for Nebulzar and the glass globe with metal, glowing leeches.

Again the world turned inside out, this time only for a moment. Kaswan realized that they were all standing above some sea on a very odd cliff face. Looking not unlike an old-fashioned tiled bathroom floor this cliff was made up of hundreds of hexagonal sized rocks.

The sound of birds, wind and waves permutated the scene. The air had a salty taste. Probably from the ocean below.

Taslasness was drawing an "imaginary" circle around them with his staff. Imaginary because no marks were left on the rocks but Kaswan was aware of a change when the circle was completed. It was like all the sounds became duller, the wind died down and the air was no longer salty.

Then his voice boomed words that Kaswan didn't understand. They sounded musical, they sounded like they changed each time he said them:

"Hoc modo ad voluntatem. Motus expromere aequora terrae huius et quicumque eam adipiscing. Quae est velle et facere dextra."

The air became static charged; it had that "after a thunderstorm" smell.

Delineni held her hand out. Kaswan took it into his hand. They all joined hands to form a circle within a circle.

The sky turned red. There was a boom, like a sonic boom and Nebulzar was in front of them, still floating on the miniature disc.

He stopped, sensing that something wasn't right:

"It's not like you to give up, Taslasness. You are playing at something."

Taslasness smiled: "The time for playing has passed, like all things must pass."

Nebulzar compelled a small rock towards them. It bounced away as if it hit the side of building: "This is your answer? I can crack your shielding easily."

"Why don't you just go away, Nebulzar? I still don't understand why you are doing any of this. All the pain you have caused, for what?"

A stunned silence came from the group as they looked towards Delineni, for it was she who spoke, not Taslasness. She was shaking with anger. Kaswan squeezed her hand and her shaking eased a little.

Nebulzar drew himself as close to the circle as he could: "I do this because you are all weak. You rely on emotion, not cold facts. You bring emotion to the Earth through your constant meddling. Idea fishes, whoever thought of that? Dreams, love and whatever else you do to keep humankind in its emotional state. Awe, wonder and creativity. This keeps you all alive, it builds your dimension. You feed off of them."

Taslasness laughed, he laughed very hard: "And you do this as a moral high ground? You are the defender of humanity?! No, let me tell you what you really are. You are a creature devoid of emotion, but there is one emotion you do feel. You are jealous; you see these things and secretly want to feel them yourself...."

Taslasness was cut off by a visibly enraged Nebulzar: "Enough!"

Hate in the form of red energy gathered in his hands.

Taslasness laughed: "I thought anger was an emotion, too?"

Nebulzar struck the circle in a brilliant red flash. Kaswan was aware of a cracking sound. He tasted the salt in the air again.

Taslasness again said the musical, changing words. Nebulzar moved to deliver another blow to the circle. Kaswan closed his eyes, knowing that this one would surly get through and kill them all.

Nebulzar let go of the red hate and in that instant, in that half of an instant; Taslasness dropped the shielding and simultaneously transformed all of them in to light. In a flash they found themselves farther up on the Causeway, looking down at Nebulzar and what was about to happen.

The red hate connected with the hexagonal sized rocks. Instead of exploding something odd happened, the energy started to dance over each point of the rocks hexagonal edges.

The energy became a rotating vortex of red sparks, growing larger and larger as it bounced off all the rocks on that part of the Causeway.

Nebulzar moved back, but too late as the vortex moved towards him. He turned to run or dematerialize as it overtook him. He fell off the disc and was sucked inside. There was a horrible howl. The vortex wobbled as if something inside it was trying to punch through it.

Taslasness and Lightener yelled "Get down!"

Everyone dropped down as a brilliant red flash and loud boom shook the Causeway.

Then there was no sound except for the birds, wind and waves.

Delineni got up. "He's gone, you did it father!"

Taslasness got up, shook the dust off: "No, not yet I haven't. Stay here, everyone."

Taslasness disappeared and then they could see that he had reappeared next to Nebulzar's disc. Lying next to the disc was Nebulzar's glass globe with the metal, glowing leeches. Within the globe a dark red liquid shook back and forth as if alive.

Taslasness raised his staff and with the bottom of it smashed the globe. The liquid within, now freed, looked to vaporize in to thin air.

An ocean away the two seniors from Keith's school paused in their wanderings. The girl, named Niamh took her boyfriend's hand in to hers: "Oisín? What are we doing?" He stroked her hair: "I, I don't know. Let's get out of here." They left their cart of meaningless things and headed back to their lives.

Back at the Causeway Taslasness smiled: "Now it is over!"

After the Storm

"The Center for Disease Control has confirmed that an outbreak of sickness earlier this week in midtown was possibly related to a new strain of the common cold…"

Lightener laughed as he turned off his "Television" orb: "Humans! You have such a knack for self deception."

Kaswan laughed as he filled his cup with more tea. He looked outside. The land was green, the sun was bright. Towards the River of Life the faint sound of musical idea fishes wafted through the air.

"So, school is starting. Can I get there from here?"

Lightener nodded: "Yes, you can get there through the gate on the hill."

Taslasness finished his scone: "Delineni, why don't you go with Lightener and Kaswan up to the hill? You can say good bye there."

Delineni nodded as Taslasness held his hand out to Kaswan and shook it:" You should stop by more often, now that you know that this place is more then just a dream."

Kaswan laughed: "I will, Taslasness, I will."

At that moment a large, grey cat jumped on the table, spilling the tea. Kaswan picked up his school stuff in a nick of time before any papers got wet. Lightener, Delineni and Kaswan walked out of the house to the sound of Taslasness scolding the cat.

They walked towards the hill as Delineni laughed:" I mean he could just clean up the mess by snapping his fingers! No need to get mad at the stupid cat for being a stupid cat."

Lightener chuckled: "You father likes putting on a good show, he always did. It makes goodbyes easier for him."

They had reached the gate. Lightener started to open it as Delineni smiled: "Well, see you later."

Kaswan kicked a stone on the ground in to a bigger stone, which deflected off with a small sound: "Yeah, be seeing you around."

He turned to walk through the gate as Delineni turned him back and gave him a hug. Both blushed as he turned back, shook Lightener's hand and walked through the gate.

Lightener was about to close the gate as Delineni told him to wait. She watched Keith/Kaswan walk away toward a red haired girl. He started talking to her as the gate closed.

Delineni just stood at the now closed gate. She was feeling something that she didn't understand. She kicked the bigger stone that Kaswan hit earlier. The stone sailed out of view.

Lightener tapped her on the shoulder: "Problems?"

She kicked another stone: "I, I don't know. Humans are weird."

Lightener smiled: "But they are wonderful, aren't they?"

"I guess."

They walked back, silently, to the thatched roof home. Finally just before entering the door Lightener tapped her on the shoulder again. "Tell your Father that I'll be back later."

Delineni nodded as Lightener held his finger to his mouth and made the "shush" sound. He motioned her to come closer and whispered in her ear: "All things in due course and time."

Then he was gone.

Delineni paused at the door, looked back towards the gate and smiled.

*FIN!

Other Works in This Series

- H.S. 1974, Awakings - Audio play, June 1974, 110 Minutes.
- The Mystery of <u>HIM</u> - Stage Play, 1975.
- The Trilogy - Short Story, 1982
- Magic - Short Story, April 1992
- The Poets Corner - March and April 1994 issues.
- Trilogy's End – Short Story, 1995
- Trilogy's End – Stage Play, 1996
- Awakings – Short Story, 2009

Who Is Kevin James Keyser?

Kevin has been writing since the early 1970's.

Kevin is the founder of the Amateur Recording Association (ARA) of Chicago an entertainment group that produced plays, audio plays, and films in the period between 1974 and 1986.

Kevin published "The Poets Corner", a monthly poetry newsletter, from 1987 - 1999. The Poets Corner is widely credited with being the first non-technical e-zine to arise during the infancy of BBSing and the Internet.

Kevin published "The Write Time", a regular newsletter about the written and spoken word from 1999 - 2000.

Kevin is a performance poet, performing on stage at a variety of spoken word venues including two performances at the Chicago Cultural Center.

Kevin has hosted poetry readings at:
- The Sun Cafe (Regular Host)
- No Exit Cafe (Guest Host)
- Cafe Aloha (Guest Host)

Television appearances:
- Songsation (1998)
- Strictline (2000)

Radio appearances:

- David Rubin, Cafe Aloha on WZRD (1998)
- Wordslingers On WLUW (2000)

Films include:

- "Search'n": A film short. "Search'n took everyday scenes and placed them to music. Shot on glorious super 8mm film and synchronized to a cassette audio track. (1977)
- "A Touch of Magic" Experimental animation storyboard. The adventures of Juniper the elf as she helps Santa bring Christmas Joy. (1978)

Videos include:

- The Final Chop: Experimental computer animation. We follow the exploits of Horance the Turkey a day before Thanksgiving. (198?)

Original Audio plays Include:

- E.D. In the year of 1973 (Pilot to The H.S. Series)
- The H.S. series (1974 –1977)
- Lonely Is The Hunter (1978)
- The Minstrel Man (1978)
- H.S. - The Metamorphosis (1979)
- The Co Ho Show (1977 – 1979)
- Radio WCLD (A.K.A. Jane Byrne and the Salt Truck Triumph!) (1979)
- Move'n On! (1979 – 1980)

Short Stories Include:

- The Trilogy (1982)
- Specter (1991)
- Trilogy's End (1995)
- Questing The Prize (1999)
- Awakings (2009)
- The Mystery of Him (2014)

Novella's Include:

- Love - The Many Eyed Beast (1988)
- A Twinkle in God's Eye (2006)

Plays Include:

- The Anatomy Of A Disk Jockey (1976)
- The Mystery of Him (1977)
- Trilogy's End (1997)

Audio Productions Include:

- H.S. The Special Tapes (1977)
- Moments of Life (198?)
- Questing The Prize (2000)
- The River - Spoken Word on CD (2002)

Current Projects:

- The Amazingly Annoying Life of Kevin Keyser – Memoir
- Poets Corner 2 – Quarterly (mostly)

Future Projects:
- Web Of Eye's – A Short Story
- The Golden Corpuscle - A Novel